UNITED FOR
UKRAINE

Copyright info
Published by Boudicca Press August 2022
Edited by Susan Norvill
Typeset by Laura Jones

Selection © Boudicca Press, 2022
Individual Stories © the authors, 2022
Cover design © Alex Thornber, 2022

UNITED FOR UKRAINE

an anthology

Edited by Susan Norvill

"Where there's hope, there's life."
Anne Frank

Susan approached Boudicca Press back in March 2022 consumed by a drive to do something to help the victims of the horrific news unfolding before us. A feeling of uselessness comes over us most when we watch such things from a distance, followed by a pulse to do something, anything to show support and make a difference.

United for Ukraine is a celebration of hope and solidarity for the people of Ukraine. It features work by writers driven to shout their words of hope, including the likes of Maggie Yaxley Smith, Fiona O'Brien, Clare Law, Margaret Beston, Linda M James and many more. It's curated with love and attention by Susan Norvill, former columnist for BBC Kent and Editor of The *Hong Kong Industrialist* in the 1990s.

Moved by the experiences of the people of Ukraine, we've gathered these collective voices to stand with the victims of these unbelievable events. Every penny of profit from the sale of this anthology is being donated to DEC Ukraine Appeal to support victims. We know it's not much.

Love and peace to you all,
Boudicca Press

INTRODUCTION

I don't think anyone can have been untouched by the horrors unfolding in Ukraine. The world watched in disbelief as Russia invaded the country in February 2022. Ordinary people were abruptly torn from their homes and their loved ones, cruelly uprooted from any sense of normality.

Amidst this emerging chaos, there were some immediate reminders of humanity: bus drivers from diverse countries on missions to Ukraine with urgent medical supplies and food, and even teddy bears for the dispossessed children; Ukrainians defiantly singing and playing music in bombed-out houses and city centres; and neighbouring countries responding with open arms, offering 'room at the inn' for exhausted refugees.

In this tragic environment, I turned to writing to express my emotions and came to realise that many others were doing the same. This gave rise to the idea of a charity anthology with Hope as the overarching theme. The contributions you'll read in this book have that in common – they are not all about Ukraine, but they are united by an element of hope.

A friend of mine said recently when talking about poetry, 'words are powerful'. I believe this power has been harnessed in the 24 contributors from across the country who have joined with me to give their time freely to this book. I want to say a huge thank you to them all – from North Yorkshire to Somerset! It has been a privilege to work with such talented writers.

I'm also incredibly grateful to the publisher Boudicca Press for believing in this project and ultimately making it a reality.

So, I hope you enjoy this collection, which has been a labour of love for us all; there really is something for everyone. If you find it to your liking, please be kind enough to spread the word as all profits from the sale of this publication go to benefit those who really need it, through DEC's Ukraine Humanitarian Appeal (dec.org.uk).

Susan Norvill, 2022

HOPE POEM

Hope is the blue on a rainy day
Blossom on the breeze
The potter's thumb in virgin clay
A caged bird flying free.

Hope is the moon on the darkest night
The smile in a stranger's eye
Hope is the flicker of candlelight
A newborn baby's cry.

Hope is the warmth of hearth and home
When all around is frost
Hope is our shield and the sword we hone
When all but hope is lost.

David Smith

WHAT THE GOLDFINCH
KNOWS ABOUT NIGELLA

Love blossomed in a mist for one steamy season,
softening the summer light.
Kissed with ragged modesty,
it swayed with a delicacy
belying its endurance.

Its appearance was short-lived.

Cool beauty soon matured,
no longer waved to be admired,
she let herself go.
Slow, swellings began to grow
within the droops of faded heads
as Love attended to the task
of making her untidy bed.

Life burgeoned out of view through the next season
in drab parchment parcels
hung among the fog,
a dreary disappointment to the eyes.
But the goldfinches knew the secrets concealed,

seeing beyond the dull disguise,
recognised the hidden force
which drew them flocking in.
They feasted on the source
of Life's black peppered energy
and warmth of the sunlight they missed.

Scarlet-flushed faces lit the grey days,
flashes of gold lifting the cold light
as they fed on the fire of last summer's Love,
leaving just enough
to flare in this year's mist.

Peppy Scott

PHOENIX

Everything dies.
The dust that was our walls
Sticks in our throats and fills our lungs.
The ash of our most precious things
Now clings to us,
Greying our hair with memories
And covering us with loss.
We are encrusted by our past.

Carrying nothing
We step across the cracked,
Naked earth that bore us.
We walk as the thunder screeches
Its parched, barren message
Over our wasted land.
We may be crushed,
But we will not be defeated.

Some things never die.
The phoenix, when it rises,
Will be a very different beast.

Andy Wallis

UNBROKEN

As rays of light illuminate frozen shards of glass,
The cathedral's soul embraces me in its fold,
And centuries' old remembrances steep the air
With spiritual paths of many human lives untold.
Ukraine's unbroken heart gives hope
To all who seek its reverent care,
Razed to ashes, cruelly bombed and blitzed,
A phoenix rises from this terror and despair.
The people with a common aim unite
To save their ravaged country from this crime,
Though persecuted, war-torn, dispossessed,
Yet praying for a different life, a different time.

Susan Norvill

THE GLOW TODAY,
THE SHADOW OF TOMORROW

Tomorrow, the idling diesel car will not choke your mind,
will not flood your thoughts like a house of black water.

For sorrow is the moon's hard bitter pill that you swallow,
the patrol of bone-birds coming to steal, riding the squall.

Tomorrow, when the wily dog comes slinking, slips in like night,
you will look deep into its obsidian eyes, give it no quarter.

Unfollow the shifting mist of paths that fall to shadow,
this map of scars that leads you blindly through the pall.

Tomorrow, if a great pillar of crows should spiral up inside to a scream,
the voices shall not harm you, they are phasms, evanescent.

No hollow too deep, there is no unlit corridor too narrow,
for you can find a way to light-foot, not to fall.

Tomorrow, you will feel no fear, only the great swim of the stream
that smoothes pebbles, calming you back to quiescence.

Come to know the glow today, the shadow of tomorrow—
find solace in the widening of stars that overarcs us all.

Paul atten Ash

THE THING WITH FEATHERS

it is hard to keep
the thing with feathers alive –
hard but cardinal

Natalie Thomas

A COLLECTION OF THINGS THAT ARE BLUE AND YELLOW

When swifts throw themselves around the high air and a single plane scratches a chalk line across the sky.

Running down the sun-cracked tractor wheel marks brushing the heavy wheat ears with my fingertips.

The bloom on blueberries eaten cold from the fridge.

My granny shows me how the white custard powder turns bright yellow when a little milk is added.

A black pearl hangs on the nib of my just filled pen; falls; blooms into deep space blue on the blotting paper.

A glowing spill held to the mouth of the test tube comes to flaming life. Oxygen present.

The roar of a Bunsen burner in the school chemistry lab. At last science seems real.

He has brought yellow roses, their wet stems wrapped in pinkish paper. 'For friendship,' he says, to my relief.

A bruise like a thunder cloud changing colour.

The flare of a match struck in the dark.

The veins my toddler traces down my wrist, wondering.

The surprising flesh of a plum under its garnet-coloured skin.

Roof slates in the rain.

Newspaper clippings saved in a scrapbook or held between the pages of a second-hand book.

A brand-new school jumper on a person who is only just four.

The centres of daisies on the school field.

A school jumper stretched over the fast-grown frame of a person who only has a few more weeks of primary school.

A banana in the fruit bowl makes a lopsided grin, as if it has something to apologise for.

The story on willow pattern plates.

Primroses jostle shyly.

A cold swimming pool, early morning.

With a gritty sound he draws out the box of overwintering dahlia tubers so I can see they have been sprinkled with flowers of sulphur against mildew.

Shadows on snow.

I didn't really know what a bergamot was when I added one to our veg box. Now I can't stop sniffing. I'm glad there are two of them.

Click-click-woomph: blue flower under my saucepan.

Hill, slick with mud and spring grass; knees and shorts and open mouths. A huge cheese truckle bounces ahead.

My granny's pale eyes look beyond me, into the past to a grandmother, mother, aunt or cousin with my voice, my laugh, my hairline, my chin.

In the garden on the corner, behind the rust-crabbed Victorian railings, they grow nothing but tall yellow daisies.

Clare Law

BREATHING IN

Hold your breath and hope.
Hold on to hope, the space between.
Between what is and what will be,
between the thing we dread
and that which we desire.
A space where time stands still.

A space where imperfection is
transmuted to a place of golden light.
Where all our outcomes are benign;
the test results are clear, the
weather holds, the cake rises,
I write a perfect poem,
the troops retreat.

Hold your breath and hope.
Endure the lifeless hour at dead
of night when all seems lost
and blackness soaks your soul.
Observe the spark in the dark,
the distant yellow glimmer of the dawn.

The troops are marching and the tanks
are slowly rumbling forward.
We go to work, and shop and eat.
The bombing starts, the skies go dark,
the sirens shriek.
We hide in cellars, sleep in bunkers,
gather weapons, barricade the streets.
The shrapnel flies, blood flows,
babies cry, civilians die.
The roads are blocked with miles
of cars as thousands fly.
We leave our homes, our jobs,
our way of life.

And even then,
when life becomes completely other
than our dreams,
we take a breath and hope.

Sue Marshall

TO YOU, FLEEING WAR

Who am I to speak to you of hope?
I live in rooms of plenitude,
and sleep in towns
where faithful night
delivers silence.

But you have come from trembling homes
where night is torn by flame and noise
and walls betray their promise.
So if you find no space for hope
among the clothes and toys and memories
swiftly packed,
then let it drop

and I shall pick it up
and keep it in a feathered box
beside a blackbird's song,
a newborn's smile,
and bluebells' twilight scent in violet glades.

And while your road is long,
while circling disbelief and grief
relentlessly uproot tomorrow,

know that in my box
your hope is safe
until the noise has cleared
and you are ready.
Then, together we will lift the lid
and watch it kiss you gently
with its rainbow touch.

Fiona O'Brien

EMILY

She cannot think of anything more beautiful:
the Pennine Chain cutting clean through England,
and Haworth standing firm; an outlying spur:
wild and windy. Flanked by the River Worth.

That morning she crosses the bridge and climbs
the narrow-cobbled streets lined with small houses;
needing to walk away from prayers and gravestones;
the sound of people; the prison of Parsonage walls.

Behind the Parsonage, through the fields - the Moors:
purple in summer sun and scoured by winds
which breathe a wilderness of furze and whinstone
into life, yet cannot move a browsing sheep.

Atlantic-driven clouds now sweep her clean
to hear the becks tumble words down rocks;
to touch their leaping thread; to feel the winds
inflate her lungs with mill-stone gritted breath.

Linda M James

FOUNDERS' DAY

Founders' Day was always busy, so before dawn Nanyamka cooked a huge batch of waakye for the holiday traffic heading to the sea. As usual she whispered thanks to the grandmother whose recipe kept a roof over Nanyamka's grandson's head, even if there was nothing left for his education. In her mind she pictured him as a doctor or a scientist, never the shoe-shine boy she knew he would become.

Everyone in the village made their living from the road but unlike the maintenance crews they didn't want to keep the traffic flowing. Their aim was to stop every single traveller, to persuade them to part with a few pesewas. Even so there was a strict pecking order: chop bar owners at the top, chichinga stallholders in the middle and finally the old women who worked right next to the road, like Nanyamka.

God smiled that day. Car after car stopped to buy her waakye. And whether customers ate it on its own or with chichinga, the first taste always drew a broad grin. By two o'clock the huge bowl on her head was feather-light, while the bag slung across her shoulder swung heavily. As the lunchtime rush eased, she realised how tired she was, but even as she acknowledged this a rusty light-blue car pulled up and three thin men got out.

"Eti sen Aunty," they said, crowding around her, looking into her bowl, patting her shoulder, eyeing her bag. She didn't like their familiarity but was eager to sell the last of her stew if she could.

"Eh-yeh," she answered, "you hungry? This is the best waakye in Volta - cheap too."

"Haba! Aunty, it's almost gone."

"Yes, it's been a good day."

Suddenly the men ran back to their ageing car, laughing, and she realised with horror that her bag was gone.

"Abeg no take my money," she shouted, but the car was already speeding off down the road.

Nanyamka collapsed in the dust and cried. Although they hadn't taken a fortune, it was still a week's rent on their corrugated shack on Futagato Street. However, her tears weren't for the money but a lifetime of humiliation. They'd laughed because she was poor, because she was a woman, because she was old. What was left for her?

And then a car door softly opened beside her.

"What's the problem, Aunty?" asked a smooth voice and she looked up at the well-dressed woman crouching beside her. An expensive looking car sat behind her, a uniformed chauffeur at the wheel. So Nanyamka explained what had happened.

"But I must buy the rest of your waakye," the woman said.

Nanyamka put the remaining stew onto a plastic plate and watched as the familiar grin spread across the woman's face. "That's it! Just like my Mama's. You have a rare gift, Aunty."

She was silent for a short while, eyes closed, before

opening them as though reaching a decision. "Will you come and cook for me?"

Michael Gutsell

IMAGINARY BANDS

At Home with Miss Hap

There were whistles and calls
For the No Luck Atolls
As they played their very first gig,
But their amp blew a fuse
Which failed to amuse
And The Fall ran away with their pig.

Mountain Rock

Otto and the Magnetic Settees
Performed live from the French Pyrenees,
Wearing Catalan masks
They sang to the Basques
And reclined to put them at ease.

Mikal Pretzel

DAY 32

from a daily poetry diary for Ukraine

32 days of bombs,
32 days of shells,
32 days of fears,
32 days of tears,
32 days of destruction,
32 days that changed the world.

32 days to give shelter,
32 days to comfort,
32 days to love,
32 days to hope for an end.

Anita Nunn

THE SUNFLOWER SEEDS

Carry these in your pocket, she said,
It's still spring in Ukraine,
Though artillery fire drowns the birdsong,
Yet this small hope will remain.

When you die, they'll live, she said,
Bruised, but uncrushed in the fray,
A golden sight for the future,
When the suffering's gone away.

Carry these in your pocket, she said,
As her eyes dilated in pain,
And the fire in her gaze condemned him,
It's still spring in my country Ukraine.

Susan Norvill

HOPE IS COMING

Blue for the bullet-pocked tractor hauling a gunmetal
tank in no man's land at midnight
Slate-blue smoke leaking from mangled ghosts of homes
that leer through concrete dust
Stone-blue rubble tripping exhausted feet, paws, hearts
Memories stuffed in bulging bags, dragged, tottering,
over ash-strewn ice, black and blue
Steel-blue eyes of the toddler clinging to her father's
damp shoulder. Be brave for me
Ink-blue darkness underground where pale frightened
faces wait
And listen
And hope

Gold for the shimmering dawn, amber scattering the
silver-blue fog
Indigo swallows dancing home over the land below,
golden bright the fields of barley the shining core
Beneath the true blue of the wide-open skies
Golden are the wild flowers blooming now, row on row
Cornflower blue and Sunflower yellow
Standing tall
Turning their faces to the light

Becky Jefcoate

HOPEFUL GARDENING FOR
THE HOPELESS

Although a keen gardener I am not the most skilled plantsman, and get easily disheartened by my failures. As well as seeing cossetted seedlings eaten by snails, flower buds snapped off by birds and veg plants producing masses of foliage but no actual veggies, I also admit to managing to kill mint, which is basically impossible.

So when I see articles saying "If you want to feel hope, plant a seed" I feel a certain amount of cynicism. What if the seed doesn't grow? What if your seedling dries out on the windowsill or you accidentally separate it from its roots when you are potting it on? What if your chilli plants are covered with compost flies and your onions are dug up by pigeons?

Sometimes hope is easily destroyed by real world experience.

Does this mean you should stop gardening, though?

I would encourage you to persevere, and here are five things to try that in my years of being an imperfect gardener always seem to fulfil their promise of making life a little more hopeful.

1. Plant a potato

No matter your level of experience, you can succeed with potatoes. Trust me, I have tried all varieties, all soil conditions, I've even picked up mouldy-looking seed potatoes with shoots poking out of the bag from a discount store and stuck them in the ground, rueing my lack of preparation. They always grow. And the joy of sticking your fork into the soil and turning up golden yellow spuds is the nearest most gardeners get to finding buried treasure.

2. Grow a geum

These happy plants seem to flourish anywhere, flowering bonnily from early spring to late autumn with little more attention than the occasional deadheading of spent blooms. They look much more stylish than the lack of effort on your part would suggest.

3. Trust in tulips

If it gets to November and you've forgotten to plant daffodils, snowdrops or crocuses, fear not: tulips are the perfect bulb for the absent minded. Stick some in a pot right up to Christmas and they will look stunning on your doorstep in spring, cheering you up every time you leave the house.

4. Encourage young growers

I've gardened with reception-age children and have seen the mess, the chaos, the total lack of respect for plants. All they want to do is take their little watering cans and flood every pot with water, right? But in a few months their peas and marigolds and sunflowers will be romping away merrily, proving that plants just really want to grow.

5. Plant a tree

Sticking a little sapling in the ground is the ultimate in hopeful gardening. You might have moved house before it's as tall as you; you might pop your clogs before it matures. But look at any tall, beautiful tree in your neighbourhood and thank the person who planted it decades or centuries ago, knowing that one day someone would enjoy the result of their little moment of hope.

Danny Webb

WHAT IF

What if mongers waged words not war,
And dropped truths; bombs be forlorn?
What if mothers drew dainty daisies,
Not IDs on backs of babies?

What if tractors towed ploughs not tanks,
And soldiers sowed seeds of thanks?
Had Satan's hate spilled not spawned,
Might more mothers mother, not mourn?

If what history whispers is true,
Wars will ebb and flow and spew,
A crimson course connecting time,
A meandering menace, a crime.

What if we seek another way,
And drain the river in Ukraine?

Gavin Rodney

HOMELAND

I grew up here
My parents grew up here
My ancestors lie beneath the soil here
I'm free here
I can choose here
I can say anything I want here
I have laughed here
I have loved here
But today I only cry here
It's my home
It's my land
It's my homeland
And you will not take it from me

Bob Francis

SWIFTS OVER TONBRIDGE

To swifts, high above the town they borrowed,
who've nothing more to harvest from its airstreams,
who've shed all images of their seasonal tenure,
of nests under eaves neighbourly with sparrows,
its lakes and intricate river systems
must resemble a smashed mirror.

Passing, as the earth tilts, into foreign airspace,
delirious with September's dying thermals,
among fluid populations who know no frontiers,
no checkpoints, no walls, their flightpaths cross
the Tropic of Capricorn, a figment visible
only to cartographers.

Oblivious, high above mountains, of altitude,
high above deserts, of mirages and sandstorms,
they reach their Thule, their Period of Cosmography,
reliving a past that never disappoints or deludes,
that never haunted them while they were airborne,
far from elephant and lion, above carparks and chimneys.

For them, only the past is not migratory.
In their minds no porous borders
blur memory and now. Sleeping on the wing,
they wake to no hallucinatory
fusion of dream and fact, to no nostalgia
for what also taunts with regrets, with past shortcomings.

Make haste, remnants of childhood, let swirls of your carefree
excitement stir again in us, as the season re-awakes
in you the coordinates of our dormant lands!
Let the air become birds, be not yet irreparably
choked with poison! Pierce us with an ache
that is the ache of warm water over icy hands!

Nick Pallot

YORK RAILWAY POND –
JANUARY 2022

The year begins
on the winter hazels
rich strings of catkins
hang buttery ripe
sparse lingering leaves
golden lanterns
lit by a gentle january sun

young shoots push through thickets
left by summer's yellow flags
that cram the margins of the pond
where mallards swim
a small flotilla gathers
sets sail disperses in peace
too early for war …

… for some at least
strident shrills silence splattered
black shadows   white flashes
two coots run on water
in furious pursuit

as a young pretender
tests territory

I watch from my warm bench
legs stretched
arms reaching out
breath blowing
fresh glows
in the kindling
of a spring

Diana Killi

THE PHOTO

A spider weaves a tapestry
in the corner. I watch it work as we wait
in the descending dusk.

So little time before you leave.

The pearl buttons on the sleeves
of my new floral dress
are hard under my fingers.
The room is too busy
with the sounds of other people.

Your uniform rubs against the satin
of my sleeve.
You uncurl my fingers,
one by one, as you turn me,
smooth as silk, towards you.

I see our love mirrored endlessly
in the smile of your brown eyes.

'Hold that pose!' The photographer says.
We do. For forty years.

Linda M James

ECHOES

A granite tapestry of life, lived in
another land, in another time.
Memories that cast shadows into
our hearts are red with flowing blood,
liquid trauma that permeates survivors.
There is no path home.
So, stitching together strands of
belonging, we weave something new,
with echoes of the past, silky soft as
the skin on my grandmother's cheeks.

Maggie Yaxley Smith

HOPE FOR UKRAINE

In the midst of war, it's not easy to think of hope, when so many forces are gathered against us. But, throughout history, wars come and go. Not to diminish the fear, the pain, the horror of it all. Not knowing what will happen next. Here is hope, that through time good will prevail.

SUN, FLOWERS AND SKY

'Blue and Yellow', go on write it: *blue and yellow*
favourite colours, a perfect combination

life seen through the lattice of the rainbow, reaching
where once again there will be love, laughter, song.

HOPE

Is Hope blind, does Hope stumble?
No. Hope is sure of foot and purpose

Hope sees through the gloom
Hope wins in spite of everything

Hope is in our blood, we live for Hope –
if we do not have Hope we are nothing.

Yes! There's always Hope – Hope endures!

THE VALLEY OF ~~DEATH~~ ~~DESPAIR~~ HOPE

How we were
once
enfolded limbs

surfaces now cold
hard…
brick, concrete, glass

prepare to fracture under pressure

when a whisper becomes a storm –
listen for the whispers…

*We stand, we stand
together!*

Steve Walter

HOPE

Blind rosebuds,
petals folded as fists,
hold last summer tight.

Cyclamen shiver
on thread-fine stems,
willow leaves spin
to shoal on the lawn –
bright yellow fish.

A Red Admiral,
sails over the garden,
a season too late.
Crows skirmish,
let loose a storm of quills.

Heaped leaves moulder
from bronze to black.
Rain blows in with the dusk.

Beneath the sodden earth –
snowdrops!

Sara Davis

AHMED –
A HERO FROM ZARZIS

While scores of small boats sit hopeless in the harbour,
you take your boat out every day, with your crew;
you throw your nets out;
you pull in a meagre catch;
you remain undefeated by dredgers
that deplete the sea of fish.

Maggie Yaxley Smith

GOLDEN SUNFLOWERS

Golden sunflowers
Facing the sun;
Tall, proud, noble
Each one.
Blooming solidarity
Symbol of peace
Shining light
For fighting to cease.
Hope clings
New growth appears
Through rumble and rock
Watered with tears.

Anita Nunn

AT THE CASTLE –
MARCH 2022

a fortress builded with embattling and strong walls

The man with the megaphone stands
in front of the Gatehouse, urges us
to spread out, to form a human chain.

We shuffle obediently, encircle sandstone
walls where kings fought and feasted
and archbishops quarrelled over ownership.

In an oasis of daffodils and primulas
the cannon last fired in Cromwell's day
is draped with the Ukrainian flag.

A tiny woman with a Slavic accent speaks
of fear for her family, her homeland. A young man
holds up a placard: *Peace and Solidarity.*

At midday we spend time in silence –
Saturday-morning-people in token splashes
of yellow and blue. Linked together. Strong.

Margaret Beston

63

WE MADE A
WORLD-SHAPED CAGE

Hope dissected on a table—
our scarlet betrayal, the entrails of human kindness.
We made a world-shaped cage,
fluttering madly within, a mist of flitting.
Fleeting scenes of love, of hate,
drunk on the honeyed promise of peace.

Hope is the distant hum
of birds never alighting, living on the wing, spent.
Unfettered as blossom, as fallout,
a nuclear quiver of winter without spring.
The night river of humanity snakes,
numbed by the prick & the sting of faith.

Hope against hope is fable—
our cities will be shelled, what's left of us, silent.
We made a world-shaped cage,
we men of blood, fit for a tyrant king.
In the Labyrinth the Minotaur waits:
once he has devoured us all, we will be free.

Paul atten Ash

I AM

the mindset to help you go forward
through nightmares in life's journey.
Even in destructive darkness,
keep me glowing in a small flicker of light.

I'm a life jacket for survival.
Some abandon me under constant, storm waves,
my light, their light vanishes.
Missed forever by those that loved them.

Whenever you doubt, feel lost, alone
reach out to the radiance of others.
Their warmth, your warmth
will make me burn brighter.

One day I'll bloom buds of peace and beauty,
new growths of happiness to bring back
dreams for the future.
My light will let them flower.

I am HOPE.

Antonia Aitken

YET

So this has happened
and the world has shifted
on its axis
yet again. I walk for hours
because I always walk
through confusion. I need
to feel the unrelenting earth reply
to my questing feet.

I am a spider's spool in wind
always somewhere unfamiliar, and yet,
the first day of the year is mild,
sunny when they forecast rain.
I watch the news footage as a dog
leaps up
on a low wall and runs its length
tail wagging
as if it were a child.

Jacquie Wyatt

TINY, RESILIENT

it's annoying, it won't let me sleep
it makes me try, though I want to weep
it causes many a censored bleep
it's a niggly, optimistic creep
tiny, resilient Hope is in me –
it makes me cope, though I want to weep

Natalie Thomas

MARRIAGE ON THE FRONT LINE

as war rumours fly
soft words are whispered
as the border is breached
they kiss and hold hands
standing shoulder to shoulder
beneath the roaring of guns

his smile meets hers
as the enemy gathers
they share their first meal
as their town is surrounded
as the shelling begins
their vows are exchanged

Sara Davis

AUTHORS

ANTONIA AITKEN started writing poetry about eight years ago and was fortunate to have begun writing with an outstanding tutor Susan Wicks, a well-known poet. Her encouragement and help gave Antonia the inspiration to continue to read and write poems which she enjoys so much.

PAUL ATTEN ASH is the pen name of Bristol-based poet Paul Nash. His poetry has been published by Deep Adaptation Forum, Envoi, International Library of Poetry, Oscillations, Raw Edge, Tandem, Tiny Seed, Understanding and Visual Verse. His poem '*Eryri*' was shortlisted in the Areas of Outstanding Natural Beauty 'Best Poem of Landscape', category of the Ginkgo Prize 2021, as selected by the National Association for Areas of Outstanding Natural Beauty in partnership with Poetry School. He has won an international poetry contest and his work has been published in anthologies *Songs of Senses* and *Memories of the Millennium.*
campsite.bio/northseanavigator

MARGARET BESTON is widely published in magazines and anthologies, most recently, *Of Some Importance, 2020, Grey Hen Press* and *New Contexts 2, 2021, Coverstory Books.* She is the author of two collections, *Long Reach River, 2014*, *Timepiece, 2019*, and a pamphlet, *When the Ground Crashed Upwards, 2020*. She is the founder of Roundel, a Poetry Society Stanza based in Tonbridge where she lives. roundelpoetrytonbridge.wordpress.com

SARA DAVIS is a member of Roundel Poets in Tonbridge, Kent. She began writing poetry on retirement from the NHS and has had poems published in the anthology *Links in the Chain*, in *New Contexts*, *South Poetry* magazine and *The Dawntreader*. She was joint winner of the Sir Philip Sidney Poetry Prize in 2020.

BOB FRANCIS has had a love of writing from an early age, mainly poems and articles. Norfolk-based Bob is also a published freelance travel writer and journalist.

MICHAEL GUTSELL lives in North Somerset. Despite dabbling for years, he only recently started sharing his writing with the world. Since then, he has been placed in writing competitions, featured on local radio, gone almost viral on the internet and been selected to study ghost story writing with Mark Gatiss. He's not considering giving up his day job yet, but he is thoroughly enjoying himself.

LINDA M JAMES is an author/optioned screenwriter/poet and a creative writing tutor who lives in Canterbury. She's had several novels, non-fiction books and poetry published: two historical novels set in WW2, *The Invisible Piper* and *Tempting the Stars*; a psychological thriller *The Day of the Swans* and a crime thriller *A Fatal Façade*. She's published two books to help writers: *How To Write Great*

Screenplays and *How To Write Great Short Stories.* Her poetry anthology, *Justice*, was published in 2021. Linda has also written two more linked historical novels set before and after WW2. Look out for *The Vienna Connection* and *Echoes of Silence* being published in 2022. lindamjames.co.uk

BECKY JEFCOATE is a creative producer based in East Anglia. Becky was previously Editor of *Stage Pass Magazine* and Director of London's Cartoon Museum. She has developed creative programmes, interpretation narratives and scripts for arts and heritage organisations including English Heritage, the National Trust, Museum of London, Bloomsbury Theatre and Royal Academy of Arts.

DIANA KILLI lives in York. A language teacher turned translator, she's been writing poetry on and off since retirement 10 years ago. New to publishing, she's had two poems published by *New Contexts 3*, *Coverstory Books* and three accepted for inclusion in *Dreich 7 Season 5*.

CLARE LAW is an editor with a creative writing practice. Her day job is editing fiction for Bloodhound Books and writing commercial content for Tunbridge Wells web developer Eonic. She blogs at *Three Beautiful Things.* threebeautifulthings.co.uk

SUE MARSHALL is a retired psychotherapist and was engaged in writing papers and books within that field. She has run regular workshops in Therapeutic Writing for many years. Sue completed an MA in Creative Writing and Personal Development at the University of Sussex in 2010. Since then, she has been increasingly drawn to writing poetry and recently joined the Crowborough Arts Poetry Group, which has given her huge support and encouragement.

SUSAN NORVILL is an editor and writer based in Kent. She was a reporter before serving as Editor of *The Hong Kong Industrialist* in the 1990s, in which capacity she also wrote speeches for members of the Hong Kong government. She worked in financial editing in the City for many years and has written a column for BBC Kent as well as contributing to various publications. She has read her poetry on local radio and is working on her own anthology.
Instagram.com/susannorvillwriter

ANITA NUNN is a psychotherapist in Tonbridge. She is part of a small writing group called the Forth Writers and a regular member of a therapeutic writing group. Anita has also participated in courses at the National Centre for Writing.
Twitter.com/AnitaSt54984401

FIONA O'BRIEN is a writer and journalist based in Tonbridge and started out on the *Kent and Sussex Courier* 'many moons ago'. She co-founded Tonbridge Welcomes Refugees in 2015 and works with refugees locally as she felt inspired by their experience.
Twitter.com/fiona_obrien

NICK PALLOT is a septuagenarian who's written a lot in the 10 years since retirement, but submitted little, as the marketplace seems rather congested. He thinks we should look up above us more often.

MIKAL PRETZEL: "Born precisely at the end of his mother's pregnancy, Mikal showed an uncanny knack for punctuality that sadly never re-materialised throughout his life. His school years happened, and no-one was ever able to adequately explain why. Some time later, but much earlier than a lot later, a slow and erratic leak of Mikal's neural by-products coalesced into pseudo-verse constructs and were mistakenly distributed to an unsuspecting group of readers." In short, Somerset-based Mikal loves writing nonsense verse!

GAVIN RODNEY is an amateur playwright and poet. His play *Arthur's on the Line* won 1st prize in the Kent One Act Play Competition, organised by the New Deal Theatre Company in collaboration with Deal Writers. He works in finance and enjoys sport and spending time with his family.
Instagram.com/groddyblue

PEPPY SCOTT writes poetry for pleasure and enjoys reading and performing locally. Her poems have been published regularly in the Kent & Sussex Poetry Society annual *Folio* and she sits on the organising committee of the Tunbridge Wells Poetry Festival. As "Pam Flitt", she appears as half of the performance duo Flitt & Folio, who offer word-based entertainment and host open mic events.
harridanswall.wordpress.com

DAVID SMITH is a writer/performer based in Tunbridge Wells, Kent. He's a regular at local events and festivals, often appearing with his performance partner, Peppy Scott, as one half of the variety double act (Pam) Flitt and (Ivor) Folio. While not generally given to submissions, David's 'proper page poetry' has been featured in a variety of publications and he is a regular contributor to the Kent & Sussex Poetry Society's annual *Folio*. He is also, for his sins, on the organising team of The Tunbridge Wells Poetry Festival. voicestw.com

NATALIE THOMAS is a poet living in Southeast England with her son and boyfriend. In 2001, she self-published her first pamphlet, *Stone*. She writes songs, posts too much to Instagram and is exploring how to make poetry for babies. Natalie was shortlisted for the 2022 Alpine Fellowship Poetry Prize. little-airplanes.com

ANDY WALLIS is a software developer by day and a keen photographer and writer. He lives in Oxfordshire with his wife, four children, and three tortoises. Together, they regularly host dog visitors.

STEVE WALTER has written for most of his life and was first published by *The Literary Review* in 1984. He's performed at the Edinburgh and Brighton Festival Fringes, based on his first book: *Fast Train Approaching...* a powerful, yet good humoured account of life during and after breakdown and recovery. His second poetry pamphlet *When the Change Came* is published by Indigo Dreams and his long poem, *Gaia 2020*, for planet Earth, is published by Making Connections Matter. Instagram.com/stevewalter8752 Twitter.com/stevewalter12

Danny Webb read English at Lampeter and worked in a variety of bookselling and publishing roles before becoming Head of Editorial at The Book People. He then moved to Yorkshire to open a successful plant shop and nursery and is now Technical Editor at JBA Risk Management. He is an aspiring author whose crime novel *The Scrap* was a winner of the Northern Noir Crime Writing competition, although he is yet to find a publisher!

Jacquie Wyatt loves an online writing competition and has won Hour of Writes 26 times and Write Invite three times. Her poetry has featured in *Ink, Sweat & Tears, South* and *High Window* amongst others, and she won the 2021 Sir Philip Sidney Prize. She is working on her seventh novel which was long listed for the 2020 Mslexia novel prize; the previous six are securely contained in a locked drawer.

Maggie Yaxley Smith MA was Head of the University of Kent Counselling Service for many years. She writes about counselling, green issues and labyrinths. Her book, *Finding Love in the Looking Glass: A Book of Counselling Case Stories* was published in 2014 by Taylor and Francis. She and her husband Chris renovated a house in Canterbury together where they enjoy family life, which includes an excited dog called Millie. She is now writing, *Counselling on Campus,* to enable students to thrive at university.

"In the face of adversity, we stand together…" Steve Walter

ACKNOWLEDGEMENTS

The biggest thanks go to Susan Norvill, who is really the machine behind this anthology, pulling the ideas and pieces together. Thank you to all the authors involved who have dedicated their time and writing for free. Thank you to the typesetters, proofreaders and printers and everyone that has been a part of this book. But mostly, thank you to you, the reader, for showing the compassion to buy this book, donating your money to DEC's Humanitarian Appeal and continuing to stand with the people of Ukraine.

ABOUT BOUDICCA PRESS

Boudicca Press is an independent publisher who celebrates the strength, courage and literary talents of women. They usually publish weird, literary fiction and non-fiction by women in the UK. Their previous work includes an anthology of weird fiction by women in the UK called *Disturbing the Beast*, and *Disturbing the Body*, a collection of speculative autobiographies about misbehaving bodies from women in the UK.

Find out more about our books at www.boudiccapress.com

DEC FOR UKRAINE

If you feel moved by any of these pieces please visit
www.dec.org.uk/appeal/ukraine-humanitarian-appeal
to donate.